The Courage Chronicles

Rainbow's End

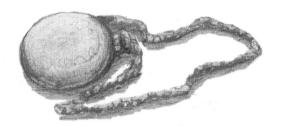

Laurie Wright

Jennifer Stables

Dedication

For the inspiration to write a better book for younger kids, thank you Paisley. For the character inspiration, thank you to my kids, Sebastien, Elise and Max (who does really like to give hugs and kisses!) *~Laurie*

To James and Myles, you are the magic in my life. *~Jennifer*

✌ CHAPTER ONE ✍

JUST BEYOND WHAT IS SEEN

"They DON'T EAT RAINBOWS!!!" Elise was stomping, yelling and getting more and more upset with her big brother Sebastien, who was doing his best to bug her. (It was working.)

After all the yelling and stomping Mom and Dad had sent them downstairs to continue their argument. They were fighting about unicorns and rainbows and all kinds of fantastical things, and their parents were sick of it.

"Go and help Max find his favorite train - please!!" Mom had begged them. Max was just two and he could be a real handful, especially during all the unpacking. As the three children made their way downstairs Elise (age 5 ½) was muttering to herself about how there were no boy unicorns, and that unicorns in general do NOT eat rainbows. Sebastien (age 9) loved to make up silly things to bug his sister about her favorite, fictitious animal, and it always worked.

The new house had three levels, and it was pretty big, which was nice. It was still *new* though, which wasn't so nice, and all three children felt unsettled. What they'd been fighting about - unicorns - was quickly forgotten for the moment at least. Elise and Sebastien were trying hard to find Max his train in their new basement, which was full of moving boxes. "Choo choo" was one of the few things Max could say, and the train was one of the only toys he'd play with for longer than three minutes.

Sebastien was trying to decide which direction to start looking in, an overwhelming decision since there were so many boxes! Giant stacks of them were all over and he didn't know where to start looking in so many piles of boxes.

"Uh ooohhh" Max said quietly, wide eyed, as one stack of boxes came noisily crashing down. The children all stopped moving and held their breath for a moment, listening to see if there would be yelling at them from upstairs.

Phew. They let out their breath after a moment had passed with no noise from their parents. Sebastien and Elise looked

around at the mess of boxes with spilled toys all over, while Max delightedly moved through the giant pile of items he hadn't seen in a while, picking things up and hugging and kissing them as he forged ahead.

Sebastien sighed as he thought about how it would most likely be HIM that had to clean it all up. It always was, because he was the oldest.

Suddenly Max was standing atop something that looked out of place to Sebastien. "Max, get off that!" he said sternly, sounding much like his Dad. The big kids slowly and carefully waded through the pile to see what it was that Max was standing on.

He had been up on a funny old suitcase, one unlike any the kids had ever seen before. It had metal corners on it, and a bright gold clasp. The outside looked like faded wallpaper with pictures of a forest land full of fairies all over it. Max had got down off of it when Sebastien had told him to, and was now fiddling with the clasp. Surprisingly, he got it open. (Max was really quite clever when it came to opening things he shouldn't be able to.)

Inside the suitcase was an interesting assortment of items. Elise pulled out an old-fashioned perfume bottle, and then held it high in the air to keep it away from Max, who was jumping at it trying to see for himself. Sebastien pulled out what looked

like an old black and white photo of some children, and quickly spun around to keep it away from Max, who wanted that too. Next, Elise pulled out a piece of paper with some writing on it.

"Read this, Sebastien!" she said, thrusting it into her brother's hands.

There is magic that lies
Just beyond what is seen;
A knowledge held only
By those who have been.

As you turn the clock's dial–
Move the hands 'round the face,
Prepare to arrive
In a new time and place.

The kids looked at each other with puzzled expressions. "What does that mean?"

Elise asked Sebastien, but he was just as confused as she was.

As they stood staring questioningly at the paper, Max started talking excitedly. "Look! Look, look!!" He was pointing excitedly at an old pocket watch that he'd found in the suitcase, which he'd also managed to open. The minute and hour hands were spinning in both directions SO quickly you could hardly see them. As the hands turned wildly around the watch face, a faint light started to shine. The children were fascinated and leaned in to look more closely. The light grew steadily stronger until it began to pour from the watch in all directions, a light so bright they couldn't see anything else in the room, so powerful that it was all the children could do to cover their eyes...

❧ CHAPTER TWO ❧

THEN SHE LOOKED DOWN

Slowly the children peeked out from their fingers as the bright light started to fade. Staring down at their feet, they noticed right away that they were standing in a meadow of lush, green grass. "What's going on?" asked Elise, turning in a circle and trying to make sense out of what had just happened. "Where are we?" As they looked around, they saw a huge forest in front of them, thick with gorgeous green trees and stunning huge red, yellow and orange flowers.

"Wane-bow!" shouted Max as he pointed to a space beside the forest and in front of them. There, starting in the grass on one side and arching up and disappearing into the sky on the other, was an unbelievably breath-taking rainbow! It was massively enormous; easily bigger than their house, and all the houses on their street put together! The colors were breathtaking and spectacular: bright glittery purple, beautiful vibrant blue, gorgeous glistening green, sunshiny yellow, delightful pumpkin orange and delicious looking strawberry red. It took their breath away to see such an amazing sight. They were standing at the rainbow's end!

Elise and Sebastien were so shocked by the incredible, giant rainbow they just stood there, staring at it. Max however, was too young to be so surprised. He giggled with delight and ran up and onto the rainbow even faster than he ran when anyone said the magic word, 'marshmallow'. Within seconds he'd gone so far onto the enormous rainbow, Elise and Sebastian couldn't see him anymore.

The bigger kids looked at each other in dismay and yelled at the same time. "MAX!" They bolted after him, towards the rainbow when they heard the sound of hooves coming from behind them at the edge of the meadow. The sound was growing louder – "Clip-clop, clip-clop, CLIP-

CLOP." They turned around expecting to see a horse. Instead of a horse, they saw a unicorn!

Elise LOVED unicorns and had read countless books with her mom about them, but nothing she had read even came close to the beauty of the unicorn that was standing before them. This unicorn's coat was pearly white – radiant and shining softly with many colors. Its mane and tail were streaked with every color of the rainbow, and a spiralling horn grew from the middle of its forehead. This was a real life, dazzling unicorn!

The unicorn was incredibly impressive to the children, but she didn't seem to be very impressed by them! In fact, she was quite upset. (Elise was reminded of what their mom looked like

when Max did something totally unexpected and a little bit bad at home, and mom blamed Elise and Sebastien for not watching him better.)

"Why did you let him ON it?!? Someone has to retrieve that child!" she said, looking distraught. Then the unicorn galloped on to the rainbow and was gone from sight just as quickly as she had appeared.

Dumbstruck, the children stood still. What had just happened?! Now they really had to go after Max! They started towards the rainbow again just as a second unicorn came galloping through the woods. His dark coat gleamed an intensely deep dark blue. His mane flowed with streaks of beautiful royal blue, sea green, and a light, glowing sky blue. Elise stared in shock! *A boy unicorn!* In a deep, angry voice he looked at the children and yelled, "Don't you DARE set foot on that rainbow!! Can't you see what's already happening?!" The unicorn gestured angrily with his head towards the rainbow.

The children had been too stunned to notice much of anything up until this point, but they turned their eyes in the direction the unicorn was referring to. One edge of the rainbow was crumbling off! It had been purple on the outside edge of the rainbow, but now the rich, glittery purple was gone and there were drops of purple dust falling from the rainbow, making a trail on the ground below. At the edge now was the color blue. What was happening to the colors?

The second unicorn was pacing back and forth and seemed to be talking something important over with himself.

Looking intently at the children he said, "I must go at once to the Oracle. She will know how to fix this horrible mess." He marched over to them and declared in a deep voice, "I am Indigar. One of you must go with me, to prove what I'll say is true." Bending down very close to them, he looked deeply into their eyes.

"I need one of you to stay here, to protect the integrity of the rainbow dust. The one with the most courage." Indigar looked them both over carefully, trying to decide.

Having made his decision, he moved right up to Elise, and touched her forehead with his horn.

"To you I give the enchantment of the unicorn. With the courage and cunning you have deep inside you, I know you will protect our sacred rainbow. Let no goblins

come near it, and do not let them collect the dust! We don't know why they want it so badly, but they have been after the rainbow for as long as we can remember."

He swung Sebastien up onto his back, declared, "There might still be time to fix this!" and galloped away before Elise could say a word.

Wait, Indigar was taking her brother, and leaving her alone? It was all happening too fast! And then she looked down.

❧ CHAPTER THREE ❧

THE ENCHANTMENT OF THE UNICORN

Elise's body started to tingle and her feet felt heavy. She had an uncontrollable urge to fall forward onto her hands. But as she looked down towards what should have been her hands, she only saw hooves! Jumping back in shock, she accidentally knocked over a glass bottle. It was the perfume bottle from the suitcase that she had been carrying in her hand the whole time. Her body was quickly transforming into something else. What was happening!!? As she frantically looked around for someone to help her, she glanced down towards her reflection in a

nearby pond. Awestruck, she moved closer. Could it be?

Elise studied her own reflection with disbelief. She wasn't a girl anymore. Not even close... she was a unicorn! Her lovely, pale, pink coat was bright and beautiful. Her mane was the same pink, with golden strands running through it. What had that dark, angry unicorn named Indigar said to her? *"To you I give the enchantment of the unicorn."* And then he'd touched her with his horn. That was it! The touch of the unicorn's horn had magically changed her into this radiant, fantastic form.

Then her ears began to twitch as they turned towards a rustling sound coming from the grass just inside the woods. *Was something in the woods?* She took a deep breath in; sure her imagination was playing tricks on her. But wait! There was something she could see from the corner of her eye, moving the orange and yellow flowers at the edge of the forest. Something was definitely there! Squinting her eyes and looking towards the forest, she saw them. At least ten small, stocky, creatures were coming towards her. Skin covered in grey scales, short skinny little legs, with dark eyes and funny noses. They looked like the goblins she'd read about in her storybooks that were usually green.

What else had she been told? '*I need one of you to stay here, to protect the integrity of the rainbow dust. The one with the most courage.*' Well shoot! That unicorn had chosen the wrong kid! Sebastien was MUCH more courageous than Elise had ever been. It was really hard

for Elise to handle things when she was afraid. She usually ran to anywhere...fast! Whatever was she going to do now? How was she supposed to protect the rainbow and its dust from these creatures?

The small black goblins continued to march towards her, and she realized she had to do something. They looked gleeful as they scurried towards the rainbow dust, barely stopping to even glance at Elise.

Elise took a deep breath and lowered her voice. "Stay back!" she told them, trying to sound scary. "I am a UNICORN!"

The goblins weren't fazed at all by her attempt at such a bold statement. They even giggled at her a little. Although Elise was now big and strong on the outside, she still felt small and frightened on the inside. She worried whether she'd be able to do anything to stop them at all!

She looked at the beautiful rainbow, and the glittery dust that kept crumbling off of it. Then she looked at her reflection in the pond again. She knew she was partly responsible for what was happening. The enormous rainbow was crumbling and it was all because of her and her brothers. Taking a few steps, she tried to come up with a plan. Accidentally she stepped on the perfume bottle from earlier.

CRUNCH.

Elise took a deep breath in and decided that even though she was afraid, she would still do her best to protect the rainbow. She reared up on her hind legs and fiercely kicked out towards the creatures. Elise was prepared to do her best and to fight if she had to.

The goblins that were steadily coming closer stopped suddenly in their tracks, pinched their noses and made pained faces. They coughed and sneezed uncontrollably. One by one they started to turn around and head back to the forest. As Elise dropped back to all four legs, the smell of perfume filled her nostrils. The smell was coming from her front hooves. They were covered in perfume from when she'd accidentally stepped on the bottle earlier. That must be what had made the goblins turn around! *Phew!*

Elise held her head high and began to trot back and forth in front of the crumbling rainbow. With one battle bravely fought and won, she was feeling more comfortable as a unicorn, and as the protector of the rainbow. On high alert in case more invaders came back towards the rainbow, she vowed to herself that she would be ready!

❧ CHAPTER FOUR ❧
MY NAME IS AURELIA

Indigar was galloping so fast it felt like they were flying! Sebastien wondering if he was dreaming, but he had never had a dream like this before. The warm wind whipped against his face as he held on tightly to Indigar's mane.

Sebastien was trying to look around as they galloped along. He wanted to have an idea of this new land they'd accidently arrived in and what it looked like. The grass was so green and lush that he thought it must have rained for a whole month to make it grow so well. *Maybe they had really good fertilizer*, Sebastien thought

to himself. *Maybe it's the entire unicorn poop!* Whatever the secret was, it was working. He had never seen grass this green before. Sebastien imagined how amazing it would feel to walk through all that thick grass in his bare feet, like walking on the wondrous carpet of nature. While riding along at breakneck speed he managed to see a few forests filled with patches of bright green leaves, growing on enormous trees. So far he hadn't seen any houses or buildings. There were no malls, grocery stores, parking lots, or vehicles either. He guessed that meant there were no people here.

As they raced on and on, he could always see the enormous, glittery rainbow stretching above him, ahead of him and behind him. It was amazing! It was also continuing to crumble into pieces and dust, which made Sebastien feel unbelievably sad.

The unicorn hadn't said another word to Sebastien, but had been muttering to himself the entire time. Finally Indigar began climbing higher up to the top of a tall grassy mountain.

Indigar stopped when they reached the peak of the mountain and Sebastien's mind went blank as he looked out at the view. It was spectacular! From the top of the green mountain, Sebastien could see for miles in every direction. Every place he looked was breathtaking and beautiful and full of color. Taking a few steps towards the edge of a cliff, he gazed out over the most perfect deep blue lake he'd ever seen.

"Hello Sebastien," said a new, melodic voice from behind him. "I know why you've come."

There was a glittering mist appearing at his feet when he turned around – a golden, sparkling cloud. The mist cleared and a towering, magnificent unicorn stepped out of it and towards him. She had a gleaming golden coat that shimmered in the sunlight and her golden mane and tail shone as brightly as the rising sun.

"My name is Aurelia, and I have been waiting a long time for today," she said.

"Great Oracle, we seek your wisdom." Indigar bowed his head for a moment, and then began to speak hastily. "The rainbow is in danger! Human children appeared at the end of the forest and..."

"I'm SO sorry!" Sebastien interrupted. "It was all our fault. We should have been watching Max better, if only he hadn't..."

"I already know," Aurelia said, stopping Sebastien's apology before he could finish it. "And all is as it should be." The oracle spoke with so much authority and certainty that Sebastien couldn't help but feel safe and reassured. "The rainbow can still be saved. To restore it you must gather all the unicorns, form the circle of courage around the end of the rainbow, and speak the ancient words. It must be done before the last color is gone. You must hurry! The color blue is already falling from the rainbow. If you don't create the circle of courage before the last color crumbles..." Aurelia's words trailed off as she looked sadly over toward the rainbow.

Aurelia bowed to Sebastien. She shook her mane, reared back on her hind legs, and disappeared into another golden, sparkling cloud.

Sebastien and Indigar locked eyes. In the dark and shining eyes of the majestic creature, he saw something that had not been there before -- curiosity, and respect.

Indigar lowered himself to one knee. Sebastien climbed up on him and away they dashed.

❧ CHAPTER FIVE ❧

NOT A COW

Max had never seen a rainbow before, and playing on top of one was the most fun he'd had in days and days. The giant, colorful rainbow made Max think of his most favorite treat - marshmallows! Walking on top of the rainbow felt like being on big, colorful marshmallows! It smelled like surgery marshmallows, too, which made him love the whole adventure even more. He bent over to give the rainbow lots of kisses, to make sure it knew how much he loved it.

Moving to a new house hadn't been much fun for Max. He missed his old room, he still couldn't find most of his toys, and his parents were cranky. But THIS was definitely fun... extremely fun! Max was just two years old. He really didn't have the words to describe the absolute glee he was feeling as he ran, jumped, and rolled on top of the giant rainbow that smelled like a marshmallow. But he didn't need words. Instead, he giggled and squealed with delight, thinking only of this moment and enjoying himself immensely.

A few times he came dangerously close to the edge of the rainbow, and to falling off, but he didn't even notice.

Iris, the rainbow-maned unicorn, noticed and was quite concerned for Max's safety. She couldn't help but smile, as she watched Max play, while at the same time as being frightened for him. Two colors had already fallen from the rainbow and she could see the next was now starting to crumble away. The rest of the rainbow was becoming more thin and weak, and she didn't know how much longer it would last, or if he'd accidently fall off the side and tumble to the ground so far below.

Iris spoke sternly, but softly, to Max. "Child, stop moving! I am coming to get you. You are not safe up here."

Max froze in his spot, looking up at her. He hadn't seen any of the unicorns until now, and he stared at her, wide-eyed but not afraid.

"Moo?" Max questioned.

"No child, I am not a cow," said Iris patiently, as she moved closer to him. "My name is Iris, I am a unicorn. We are unique to this land, though there have been many books written about us in yours."

Max was trying hard to say 'Iris', but it was causing his mouth some trouble to get out.

Iris kneeled down in front of Max, and looked at him adoringly. How charming was this small human child, trying so hard to get the right words out. She couldn't be angry with him. He hadn't known what effect his footsteps on the rainbow would have. *I must get him to safety*, she thought.

"Child, climb on. We will ride!"

"Ride? Ride!!!!" Max knew what 'ride' meant (he often climbed on his brother and sister for a horsey ride) so he clumsily, but excitedly climbed onto Iris' back and clung to the beautiful rainbow colored mane, now streaked with a dull, plain, light gray where the colors purple and blue had been.

Together they easily jumped over the edge of the rainbow, just as the color green began to crumble away into glittery drops and dust.

"Come, child. I will show you a bit of our land before I return you to the others. Hang on tight!"

⤋ CHAPTER SIX ⤌

THE ONE WITH THE MOST COURAGE

Elise was beginning to enjoy guarding the rainbow. She felt large and strong and brave. With each step she took her confidence grew. Maybe she would enjoy staying a unicorn forever! At the same time as feeling happy about her newfound strength, she was feeling really badly about the rainbow crumbling. Three colors had now crumbled away, and there wasn't much time before the entire thing would be glittery dust on the ground. Imagining what the world would look like with no color in it brought a tear to Elise's eyes. She desperately wished that the rainbow would stop crumbling.

Once again, Elise's ears began to twitch. *Oh no, what now?* There was a rustling noise coming from the edge of the woods and Elise was immediately on high alert. It was easy now that her hearing and sight were a hundred times better than when she was a human.

Her attention was focused on the edge of the woods. When the children had arrived, they had been bursting with a variety of stunning colors. Emerald green leaves on the trees, a warm, browny-green moss had covered the tree trunks, and the grass had been a welcoming and vibrant lush carpet all around the rainbow's base and trailing into the woods. Now everything that had been so beautiful and green looked gray and drab, and it was heartbreaking to see it.

Her unicorn senses were sharp, and again there were some movements in the tall grass. She scanned the tree line for any motion but didn't see anything except the leaves swaying in the breeze. Wait! What was that? There was a movement in the tall grass in front of the trees… yes! There to her right. Now she could clearly see them and the beastly little goblins were coming toward her again!

The last time the goblins had been repulsed by the smell of the perfume, but she couldn't be sure the scent was still strong enough to repel them. Each one of them was heading for the end of the rainbow, looking intently at the dust on the ground and carrying a small leather pouch slung over their shoulder. *They must be using the pouches to gather the dust,* realized Elise. Which meant this time they were coming prepared.

For a moment Elise wanted to run away. There were at least ten of them, and only one of her! She could feel her heart pounding in her chest. *I am just a little girl,* she thought fearfully. *How can I face so many goblins on my own*? Elise wanted to call for her parents, to cuddle up with them and hide in their arms. She really wanted to go home.

Then Indigar's voice rang through her head. *"The one with the most courage."* He had looked both children over quite closely, and he had chosen HER. Indigar had touched her with his horn and magically transformed her. He had seen the courage within her, now she just needed to see it within herself. Being courageous didn't mean you weren't scared. It meant you did what you had to do, even when you were scared. She looked down at her hooves and felt a surge of strength move through her, from the tips of her toes up to the tips of her ears. She raised her head and stared directly at the goblins. *I can do this,* she thought bravely to herself.

"Stay BACK! I am NOT scared of you. NO ONE will touch that dust while I am guarding it!!" She reared back on her hind legs again, hoping that the perfume smell was still strong enough to make them run away. The goblins wrinkled their noses and made some funny, grossed out noises, but they didn't run away like the last time.

Drat.

Elise had really hoped the perfume would work again, but now she would actually have to fight. There was no feeling of fear anymore, though. Now she felt sturdy, tough and powerful. Elise the Unicorn was going to protect this rainbow. No. Matter. What.

The goblins came closer and closer, chattering to each other and talking gibberish, while gesturing from Elise to the rainbow and back again. They weren't scared of her at all! In fact, they came so close to her she could almost kick them. *Hmmmmm.*

Giving them one last chance to leave peacefully, Elise narrowed her eyes and forcefully yelled, "IF YOU COME ANY CLOSER I WILL STOMP ON YOU AND TURN YOU INTO A PANCAKE!!" To emphasize her point she lifted one front hoof and stomped on the ground with all her might. The ground shook and a shock

wave spread out from where her hoof had landed on the ground. Amazed, she watched as the wave travelled all the way to the creatures and past them into the woods. Some of them stumbled and fell down, and some tripped on others while trying to get away from her. They scrambled to their feet, looking at Elise with both fear and awe. Their legs scurried quickly to get away from the courageous unicorn and they raced in alarm back into the woods.

❧ CHAPTER SEVEN ❧

LISTEN, MY FRIENDS!

Sebastien and Indigar slowed down when they reached a large, dreary clearing that would have been a glorious green before. Indigar wasn't blue anymore. His coat that had been lustrous and beautifully dark blue was now dull and gray. The color in his mane, which had been streaks of beautiful blues and greens, was now washed out and lusterless.

A crowd of around twenty unicorns gathered around them. Many were completely colorless, sad and dreary looking. Some had all of their color still and really stood out from the crowd, making the gray, dreary unicorns seem even more heartbreaking. A cloud of sadness surrounded the unicorns, as though their happiness was fading along with the crumbling colors.

"My friends!" Indigar called, "We have an emergency! Three human children have come to our land, and the smallest child climbed *on* to the rainbow! This is why the rainbow is crumbling and our colors are fading. It is in great danger of disappearing completely - we all are!"

There was a rumble of voices from the crowd. "Children?" they whispered. Quickly their sadness turned to outrage and they began to approach Sebastien while shaking their heads back and forth, angrily.

Sebastien was preparing to apologize and take total responsibility for the situation, when Iris and Max came galloping into the clearing and stopped abruptly next to them. Her mane wasn't the same vibrant rainbow of colors that it had once been, it was quite dismal actually. *"The colors are fading so quickly!"* thought Sebastien. *"We have to save the rainbow, and fast!"* He looked down at his clothes. The color was even fading from them! Then he really thought hard about it – the color purple had fallen from the rainbow. Now everything that was purple had turned to gray. The blue on Indigar and the blue from Sebastien's jeans had turned to gray. There was still grass in the clearing, but it no longer held any color. The only colors left on the unicorns were the ones that were left on the rainbow - red, orange and yellow.

'The colors that are falling from the rainbow are the colors that are disappearing. The rainbow controls all of the color throughout the land, and without it everything will be drab, dull and gloomy. No wonder the unicorns are so worried!' Sebastien thought with sadness.

The mob of angry, gray unicorns whirled around to look at the new arrivals. Max clapped his hands, excited to see so many magnificent new friends. But the unicorns weren't happy to see Max, and he could sense it. "Off" he said, in a small, pleading voice. He tugged on Iris's mane. She kneeled on the ground, allowing him to easily get down.

Max looked at the unicorns with wide eyes. He went around to each of them, one at a time, hugging their legs and giving each one a small kiss. He babbled as he hugged them, and although they probably couldn't understand what he was saying, it seemed that all of the unicorns understood what he meant, and forgave him. Max was trying to say he was sorry.

When Max was done making amends (and friends) he looked at Sebastien. "Bas-ten!" cried Max. Open-armed, he scampered to Sebastien as fast as his little legs would go. Sebastien wrapped his arms tightly around his baby brother. He was surprised by how relieved he was to see Max, safe and sound. They hugged each other fiercely, and Max kissed his big brother on the belly and the back and the arm and everywhere he could, until Sebastien gently pulled him away.

"I'm so happy to see you Max! You shouldn't run away from us like that, ever again."

Indigar was becoming impatient. He cleared his voice and said loudly, "Listen, my friends! We have spoken to the oracle and know what we must do. We need to gather around the rainbow and form the Circle of Courage. Then we must join our voices and say the ancient words. We MUST restore the rainbow before all the colors disappear!"

The crowd agreed and huffed with excitement. They pawed at the ground, shaking their manes and flicking their tails.

Sebastien climbed on top of Indigar again after helping Max climb back onto Iris. Humans and unicorns raced off towards the end of the rainbow, together.

❧ CHAPTER EIGHT ❧

RESTORE OUR PRECIOUS LIGHT

As a group, the unicorns and the two human riders charged through the dull gray grass. Yellow drops and dust could be seen falling down from the rainbow, and making a glittery trail of yellow dust below it. There wasn't much time left! The group stopped at the end of the rainbow just in time to see a pack of frightened goblins scurrying away from a powerful unicorn. Sebastien was concerned about Elise, where had she gone? Indigar called up to Sebastien and said, "So much courage there, your sister is impressive!" Now Sebastien was really confused. What on earth was Indigar talking about? Elise was nowhere around.

All of a sudden he remembered what Indigar had said to them when he'd first appeared, and had been so upset. *'I need one of you to stay here, to protect the integrity of the rainbow dust. The one with the most courage.'* Then he had touched her with his horn, before taking Sebastien and rushing away. Sebastien looked at the powerful unicorn again, stared intently into its bright and beautiful eyes, and at the beautiful pink colored mane and tail, with glittering streaks of gold running through it. There was no question now. This formidable, majestic unicorn was his little sister. He'd never admit it, but he was impressed.

"Elise!" He shouted to her, "We know how to save the rainbow!"

The herd of dismayed unicorns gathered at the end of the rainbow and grew silent, as they sadly stared at the two colors that were left. Were they too late? Could the rainbow still be fixed? Helplessness and despair overtook them and they stopped moving. All hope was leaving them as they watched the orange crumble to dust in front of their eyes, and the same color from the flowers and themselves fade to gray.

Sebastien looked at Elise and they locked eyes in silent agreement. He went over and stood next to her, placed his hand on her back, and drew strength from her. "Listen to me! The rainbow **can** be saved, but we need to focus and we need to act fast! The oracle Aurelia said all unicorns must join together and form the Circle of Courage and then say the ancient words." He tried to sound important, and to spur them into action, but it wasn't working. They were still rooted to their spots, heartbroken and unmoving.

"Elise!" He looked at her and begged, "DO something!!" Elise was one of them now; maybe they would listen to her.

Elise was the only unicorn with color that hadn't faded or turned gray. She gleamed next to all of them, and it was impossible to look away from her. Holding her head high, taking a deep breath, and stomping her front leg like she had done to scare off the goblins (only not quite so hard) she concentrated on sending a small shock wave through the crowd, and it worked! Now they were really paying attention to her. In her loudest and most powerful voice she yelled, "LISTEN TO ME!!! It is up to all of us to work together to SAVE the rainbow. This will NOT be the rainbow's end! True courage is about acting as you know you must, even when you are sad or scared. Now, make a circle!" Like a true unicorn hero she was speaking forcefully, and because of her inspiring words the other unicorns started to move. Elise pointed them each to the spots they should go, and they started to form a large circle around the base of the rainbow and the one color remaining - red. Time was almost up.

Elise motioned to Sebastien to get on her back. Iris stood beside them, now mostly a dull and lusterless gray, carrying Max on her back. Something stirred inside Elise. A flood of words was coming to her. Even though she had never heard the ancient chant, she knew exactly what to say. As soon as she began to speak, the other unicorns joined in.

Rainbow strong and true
That shines from red to blue
Let our hearts burn bright
Restore our precious light

Elise felt a change come from inside her, and her horn began to glow. Sebastien had to look a few times at her to make sure that what he was seeing was really happening. Max's mouth had dropped open and he pointed at her head. Elise's horn glowed stronger and then a curl of orange glowing light sprang from her horn around to all the other unicorn's horns, and then finally curled up onto the rainbow. With what looked like a fireworks explosion of glitter, the orange was restored!

Max whispered, "Again!" and Elise began the chant a second time. Just like before, her horn glowed, but this time it glowed with a yellow light. The light jumped from her horn to all the others, and then up to its proper spot on the rainbow. The unicorns were excited now! They could feel the ancient magic moving through their bodies. They chanted even louder and faster than before, and this time

Sebastien and Max spoke the ancient chant as well:

Rainbow strong and true
That shines from red to blue
Let our hearts burn bright
Restore our precious light

Each time they said the chant they watched a new color return to the rainbow – green, then blue, and finally purple. As the last bit of purple was restored, there was a HUGE explosion of fireworks in the sky. Glitter bomb after glitter bomb of all different colors were going off in the sky above the rainbow, with loud 'POP' 'POP' 'POPs!' going off with the glitter explosions every few seconds.

Everyone breathed a sigh of relief and smiled at the same time. The tension and sadness that had been present in the air a few minutes before was gone now and replaced with an atmosphere of joy. The unicorns reared and pranced, neighing happily. There was much hugging, dancing and merriment between the three children, and of course, many kisses from Max.

All of a sudden a fantastic golden mist began swirling in front of the three children.

❧ CHAPTER NINE ❧

YOU MAKE A WONDERFUL UNICORN

The golden mist swirled around, growing faster and wider as it turned. Then, from out of the mist stepped a glowing golden unicorn. Silence fell over the herd of unicorns as they leaned forward on bended knees. Sebastien nodded his head towards her, Max looked like he might hug and kiss the Oracle, and Elise bowed her head and lowered herself to bended knees as the other unicorns were doing.

"Bravo, everyone! I am not surprised at your success, but I am also quite relieved." Aurelia walked over to Elise and bowed in front of her. Elise was so surprised she didn't know what to do. She looked up into the Oracle's deep brown eyes, and the Oracle spoke to her.

"Please, get up, you shouldn't be kneeling. It is I who should be kneeling to you! We are indebted to you. Your bravery and magic kept the goblins away from the rainbow dust. If they had managed to get it, it would have meant the certain end of the rainbow. Have you guessed why this rainbow is so very important to everyone?" she asked Elise.

"The rainbow gives this land its color... and it controls the color in our world too, doesn't it?" Elise guessed. Watching the colors around her fade away from the rainbow, grass, the flowers, and the unicorns had made her feel unbelievably sad and heavy-hearted.

"Yes you are correct. If our rainbow were to completely crumble, every color in our world would disappear, and in your world too, all the color would be gone forever." It looked like the thought of this possibility really disturbed the Oracle. She wasn't smiling as she paused to look around her, at the land, the forest and the unicorns. Her voice sounded sad as she continued. "We are thankful you came here. The truth is it was not your brother that caused the rainbow to crumble, although he did speed up the process. It had already started happening before you arrived, and I am not sure we would have been able to restore the rainbow on our own. You truly are a remarkable girl, Elise. You showed true courage by acting bravely even though you were scared."

Turning to Sebastien she said, "You, too, showed great courage. You were honest, willing to help strangers and willing to take a chance when you needed to."

Looking down tenderly at Max she said, "And a delightful little creature you are! Adventurous and full of joy, we will miss you, and your hugs and kisses, too. So much strength lives in each of you. I am so proud of what you did here, please remember that when you leave." Walking close to Elise, Aurelia dropped her head to Elise's ear and lowered her voice so only she could hear. "You make a wonderful unicorn, but you can not stay one forever. When you go back to your world, you will be returned to your true form, but with a token of your time here."

"Farewell children! We thank you from the bottom of our hearts." Aurelia said to them all, appreciatively.

The three kids all went around saying goodbye to the unicorns. Max, of course, gave plenty of hugs and kisses. When they were done their goodbyes, they went back to Aurelia the Oracle.

Sebastien was wondering how they would actually get home, but he didn't have to wonder long, because Max took the pocket watch back out of his pocket, where it had been all along, opened it and started to play with the dial. It started to glow and light poured from the watch in all directions, a light so bright they couldn't see anything else. Once again the light was so powerful it was all the children could do to cover their eyes.

❧ CHAPTER TEN ❧

SPAGHETTI AND SAUCE

As the light slowly faded, the children peeked out from between their fingers. They were back in their new home, in the basement. Everything seemed to be just as they'd left it. In other words, a great big mess from where the tower of boxes had fallen over.

"Did that really happen?!" asked Elise, looking around. Sebastien looked at her and pointed.

"You're YOU! You're you again! What a terrific unicorn you were but I'm SO glad you're YOU. Where'd you get the necklace?" He was pointing at her neck.

"I am? I am!! Being a unicorn was really cool, but I'm super glad to be me again." she said as she patted herself all over, and looked at her fingers and her toes. She touched the necklace and lifted the crystal hanging from it up to get a better look. It was pearly white and absolutely stunning.

"Wow," Elise sighed. As she turned it around trying to see it from all angles, the crystal seemed to glow a bit from the inside. "Gorgeous."

"We should go tell mom and dad that we're all right." Sebastien suggested, reluctantly. "We've been gone for so long, I bet they're really worried. I hope they didn't call the police, or Gramma! This will be SO hard to explain."

Max started to head for the stairs making hungry noises. "MMmm.... Yummy Getti!!" he said, and continued making the 'Mmmm' noise as he went up the stairs heading for the kitchen.

"Sebastien, wasn't Dad starting dinner when we left? Spaghetti and sauce?" asked Elise.

"Yeah, I think he was!"

The kids gave each other a big smile. No time had passed at all at home! They wouldn't have to explain anything after all. *Phew.*

"Sebastien, what did she mean? She said that Max didn't cause the rainbow to crumble, and she looked so worried!" Elise had a troubled expression on her face.

"I'm not sure, but I've been thinking about it too. What would make a rainbow crumble like that? I guess we'll never find out, now that we're home." Sebastien and Elise each stared in the direction of the old suitcase for a few seconds, lost in their own thoughts about the rainbow's end.

"You know, you were really brave against those goblins. You made an awesome unicorn." Sebastien gave his sister a genuine smile, filled with admiration. And then, because he couldn't resist, "See? I told you there were boy unicorns."

Elise laughed at her silly brother who always thought he was right. "Yes, I guess you were right about that. But they definitely DO NOT eat rainbows!" Elise and Sebastien gave each other a few playful nudges, and headed up to eat together. They were starving!

❧ ABOUT THE AUTHORS ❧

Laurie Wright- Laurie is a speaker, author, and educator who is passionate about helping children increase their positive self-talk and improve their mental health. Laurie speaks to parents, teachers, has given a TEDx talk, created resources and has written 2 books, all to further the cause of improving the self-esteem of our children. Laurie is a huge advocate for children's mental health and works every day to improve the way we interact with kids, to help them learn to handle all of their emotions.

Jennifer Dale Stables- B.F.A, B.Ed.

Illustrator and contributing author, Jennifer Dale Stables, is a passionate artist and educator. A former classroom teacher, Jennifer has dedicated her artistic endeavors to creating artwork and illustrations for children, and teaching art in schools throughout Alberta. Through her business, Jenny Dale Designs, she creates whimsical artwork and writes poetry to accompany each one of her lovable creations. Rainbow's End is Jennifer's eighth published book.

Made in the USA
Middletown, DE
10 March 2018